*For Connor, who loves balloons, and for
Mrs. Nutter, Harry's favorite math teacher*

W. U.

*

To Danylo and Antonina

L. K.

Text Copyright © 2010 Wendy Ulmer
Illustrations Copyright © 2010 Laura Knorr

Sleeping Bear Press®
315 E. Eisenhower Parkway, Suite 200
Ann Arbor, MI 48108
www.sleepingbearpress.com

© 2010 Sleeping Bear Press is an imprint of Gale, a part of Cengage Learning.

Printed and bound in China.

First Edition

10 9 8 7 6 5 4 3 2 1

Library of Congress Cataloging-in-Publication Data

Ulmer, Wendy K., 1950-
Zero, zilch, nada : counting to none / written by Wendy Ulmer ;
illustrated by Laura Knorr.
p. cm.
ISBN 978-1-58536-461-9
1. Counting — Juvenile literature. I. Knorr, Laura, 1971- ill. II. Title.
QA113.U46 2010
513.2'11 — dc22   2009037412

ZERO*ZILCH, NADA

Counting to None

Written by Wendy Ulmer

Illustrated by Laura Knorr

Harry was so excited. Today was the first day of his new job. He was going to work in the 4 Color Balloon Factory. Harry loved, LOVED, LOVED balloons!

"Good morning, Harry," said Mr. Huffy. "Your first job is to blow up **100** balloons for Mrs. Doopido's birthday party. I'll stop in later to see how you are doing."

Harry looked around the room where Mr. Huffy left him. There was a big box of floppy, deflated balloons. There were **10** long balloon-bunching stations, each with **10** slots to hold a balloon. Harry picked up a yellow balloon, took a deep breath and began his new job. Puff, puff, puff—tie it in a knot—add a nice long string—slip it in a slot. Harry picked up a green balloon, took a deep breath and puff, puff, puff—tie it in a knot—add a nice long string—slip it in a slot.

A balloon a day keeps the blues away.

All morning Harry blew up balloons—
yellow ones, green ones, then a blue one and sometimes a red one.
All morning Harry sang the little song,

puff

puff

puff

tie it in a knot

add a nice long string

slip it in a slot.

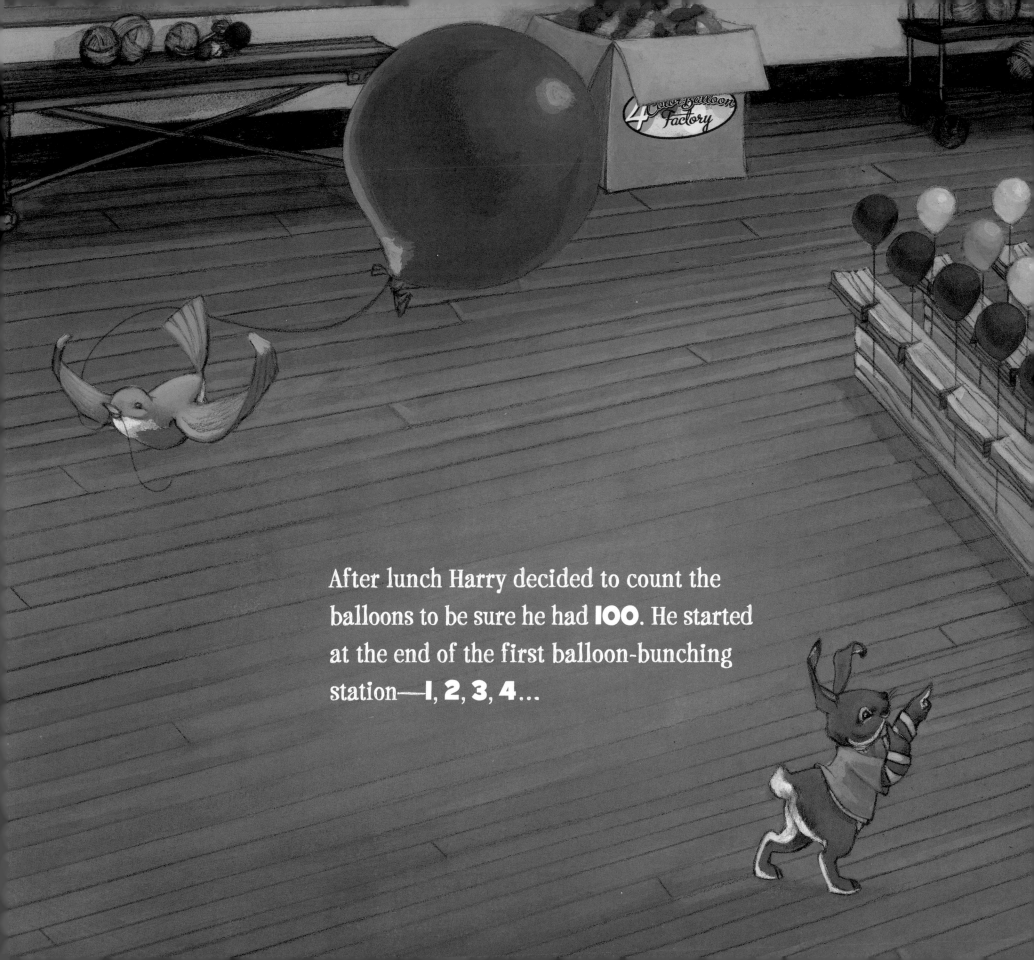

After lunch Harry decided to count the
balloons to be sure he had **100**. He started
at the end of the first balloon-bunching
station—**1, 2, 3, 4**...

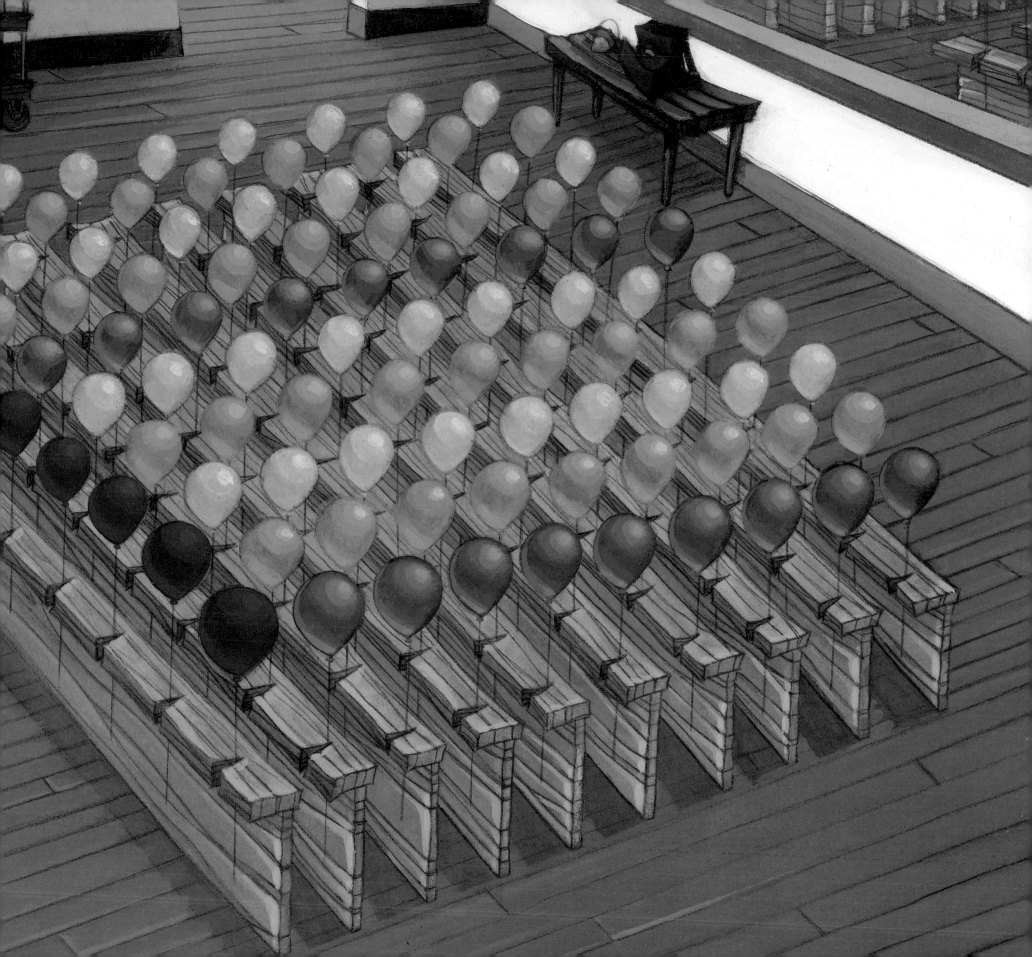

"What are you doing, Harry?" asked George, who was delivering a new box of yellow balloons.

"I'm counting to make sure I have **100** balloons," said Harry. "But now I will have to start again because I lost count."

"Harry, just count the red ones on the ends by tens. Whenever you count a red balloon, it will be the same as counting **10** balloons. That will be faster."

"Ok," said Harry, "I'll try that! **10**, **20**, **30**…wait. Did I count that red one over there? I'll start again—**10**, **20**, **30**, **40**… oh my…I don't remember where I started."

"Harry," said George, "You can just…"

"No, wait, I know how to keep my counting straight!"
Harry picked up something shiny from the floor and
started to count the red balloons again.

"**10** (pop), **20** (pop), **30** (pop),

40 (pop), **50** (pop), **60** (pop),

70 (pop), **80** (pop), **90** (pop), **100** (pop)!"

"I do have **100 balloons!**" Harry shouted.

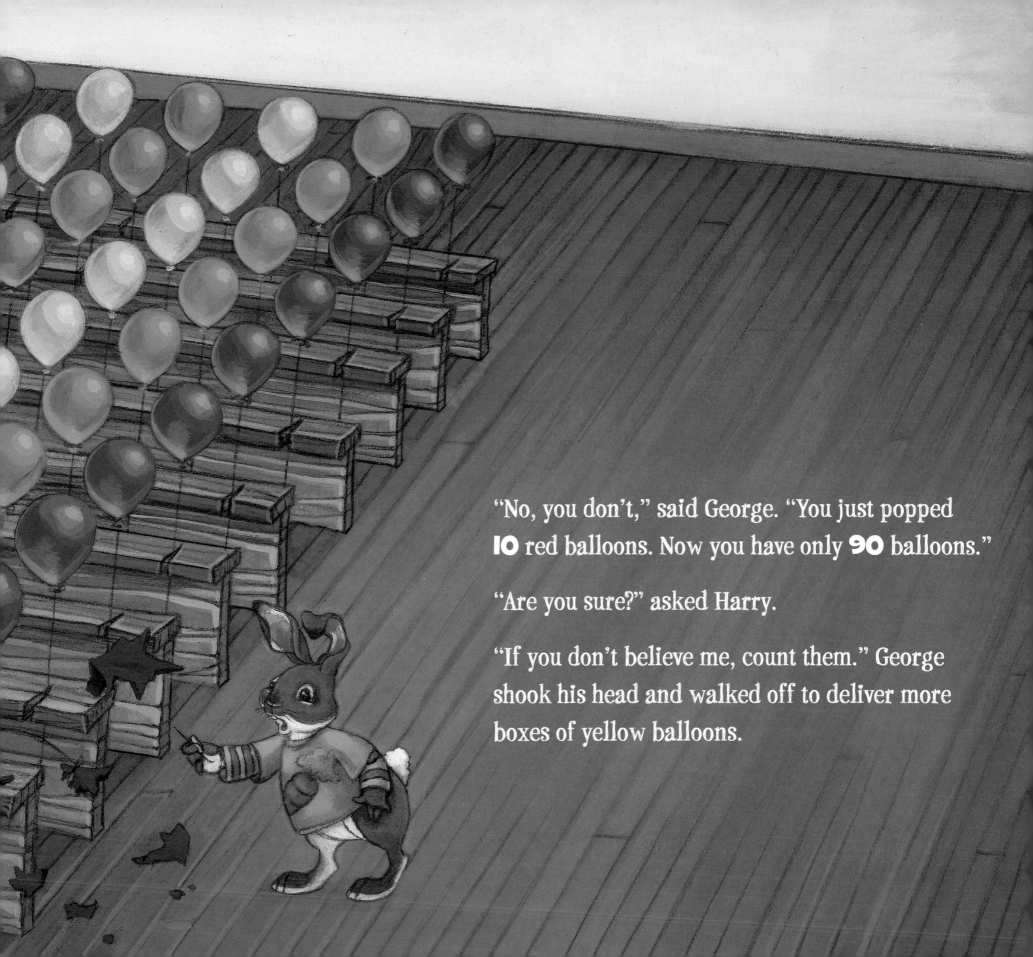

"No, you don't," said George. "You just popped **10** red balloons. Now you have only **90** balloons."

"Are you sure?" asked Harry.

"If you don't believe me, count them." George shook his head and walked off to deliver more boxes of yellow balloons.

Harry began counting again at the end of the first balloon-bunching station—"**1**, **2**, **3**, **4**..."

"What are you doing, Harry?" asked Marcie, placing a new ball of string next to a box of balloons.

"I'm counting because George says I have only **90** balloons," said Harry. "But now I will have to start again because I lost count."

"Harry, just count the blue ones by fives. Whenever you count a blue balloon, it will be the same as counting **5** balloons. That will be faster."

"Ok," said Harry, "I'll try that! **5**, **10**, **15**...wait. Did I count the blue one over here? I'll start again—**5**, **10**, **15**, **20**... oh my...I don't remember which row I counted first."

"Harry," said Marcie, " just start at..."

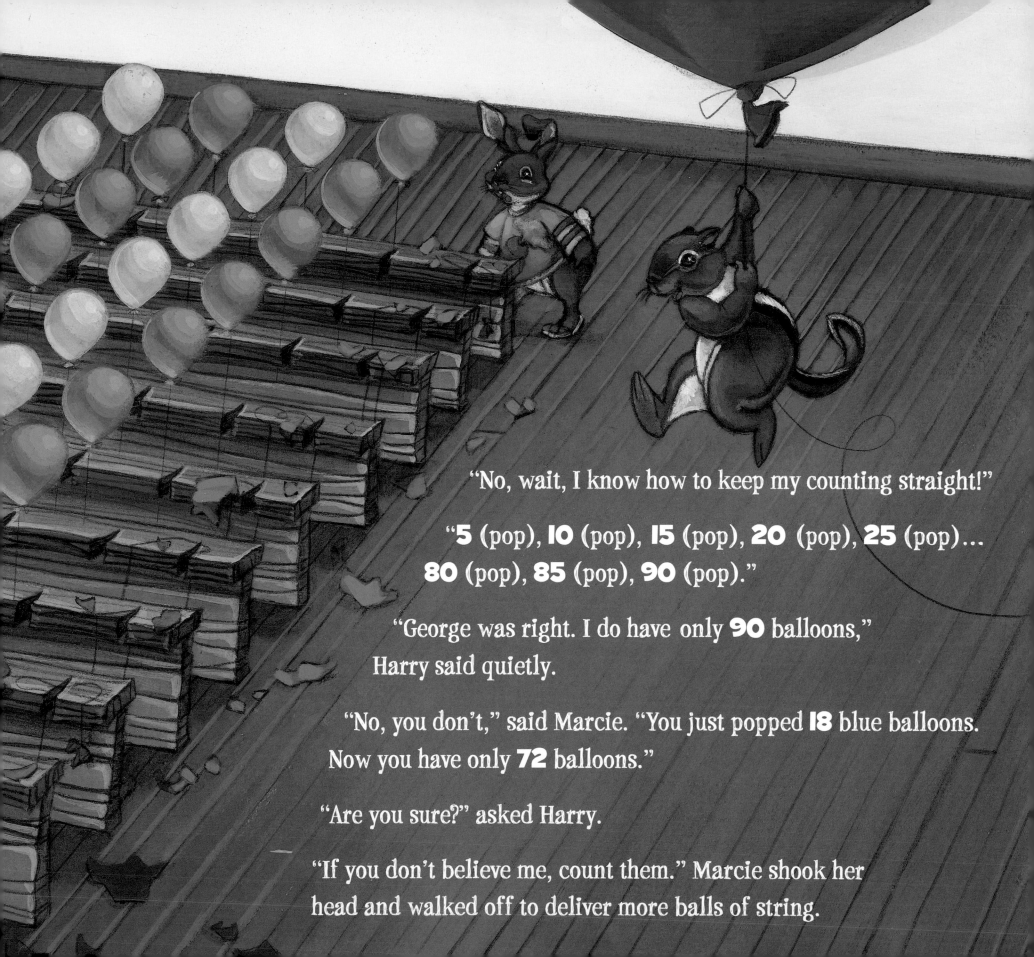

"No, wait, I know how to keep my counting straight!"

"**5** (pop), **10** (pop), **15** (pop), **20** (pop), **25** (pop)...
80 (pop), **85** (pop), **90** (pop)."

"George was right. I do have only **90** balloons,"
Harry said quietly.

"No, you don't," said Marcie. "You just popped **18** blue balloons.
Now you have only **72** balloons."

"Are you sure?" asked Harry.

"If you don't believe me, count them." Marcie shook her
head and walked off to deliver more balls of string.

Harry began counting once again at the end of the first balloon-bunching station—"1, 2, 3, 4…"

"What are you doing, Harry?" asked Joe, who was on his way to the Shipping Department.

"I'm counting because Marcie says I have only **72** balloons," said Harry. "But now I have to start again because I lost count."

"Harry, just count the green ones by twos. Whenever you count a green balloon, it will be the same as counting **2** balloons. That will be faster."

"Ok," said Harry, "I'll try that! **2, 4, 6**…wait.
Did I count that one twice? I'll start again—**2, 4, 6, 8**…
oh dear…I don't remember where I began."

"Harry," said Joe, "just put a box at the end where…"

"No, wait, I know how to keep my counting straight!"

"**2** (pop), **4** (pop), **6** (pop), **8** (pop), **10** (pop)…
68 (pop), **70** (pop), **72** (pop)."

"Marcie was right. I do have only **72** balloons,"
Harry said sadly.

"No, you don't," said Joe. "You just popped **36** green balloons.
Now you have only **36** yellow balloons left."

"Are you sure?" asked Harry.

"If you don't believe me, count them." Joe shook his head
and strolled off to the Shipping Department.

Harry stood at the end of the first bunching station.

"This time I will only count them once," declared Harry.
"**1** (pop), **2** (pop), **3** (pop), **4** (pop)...
34 (pop), **35** (pop)...

"HARRY! WHAT ARE YOU DOING?"

Mr. Huffy looked upset.

"**36** (pop)."

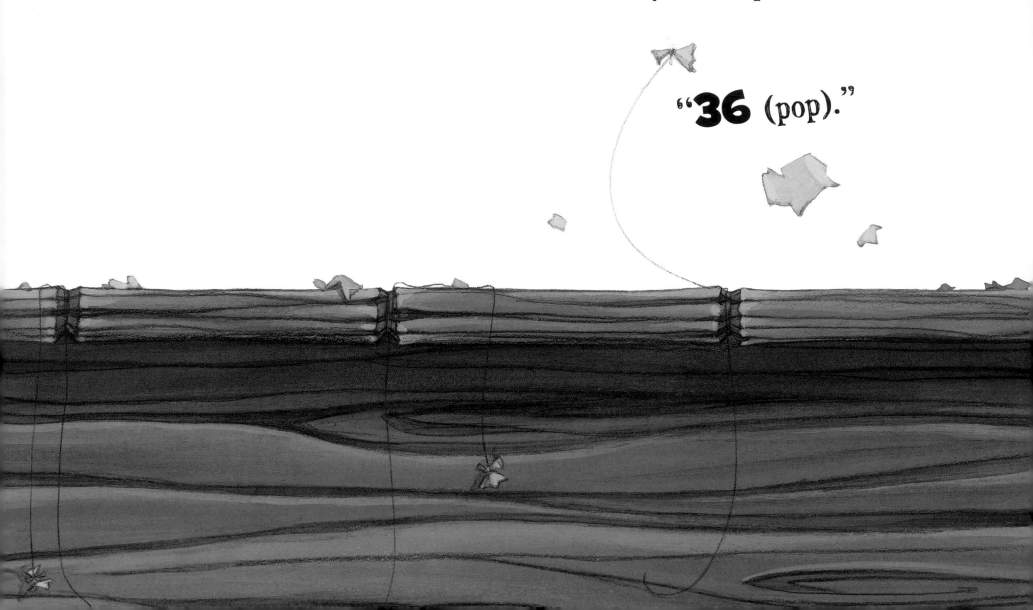

"Where are the balloons for
Mrs. Doopido's birthday party?"

"I tried to count them, sir, but George told me to count by tens and I got confused, and Marcie told me to count by fives and I got confused, and then Joe told me to count by twos and I still got confused, and now I see I counted to none," Harry whispered.

"Oh, Harry," smiled Mr. Huffy. "It's much easier than all that. There are **10** balloon-bunching stations and each station has **10** slots. **10** stations with **10** slots— **10** sets of **10**—**always equal 100**."

"Always?" asked Harry.

"Always. But now I'm afraid you will have to start all over again."

"That's alright," smiled Harry.
"I'll have it done in a song."

puff

puff

puff

tie it in a knot

add a nice long string

slip it in a slot.